27.02.01

Dear Finn,

This beautiful book contains
stories of the great Irish
legend Finn (Fionn) Mac Cumhail
who you're named after. He was
a brave & courageous boy who
stood for honesty, truth & loyalty.
May you be just like
that.

Very best wishes
Your Irish friends
Siobhal & Rebecca

MW00978599

## This Poolbeg book belongs to:

Finn

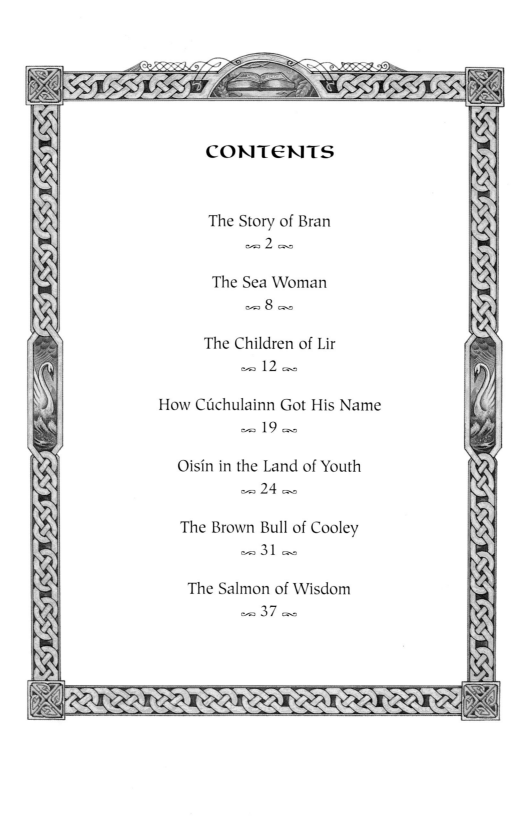

# CONTENTS

# FAVOURITE IRISH FAIRY TALES

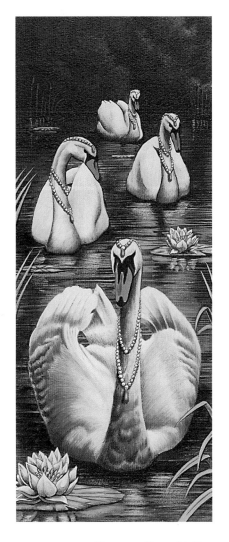

## SOINBHE LALLY

### ILLUSTRATED BY
# FINBARR O'CONNOR

POOLBEG

# THE STORY OF BRAN

The younger sister of Fionn Mac Cumhaill's mother was very beautiful. She married the chief of the Fianna of Ulster but did not know that her husband had already promised his love to a fairy woman.

When the fairy woman heard of the marriage she was jealous. She stole the new bride away and cast a spell on her, turning her into a hound. While the enchantment lasted, the hound gave birth to two pups.

Fionn found out what had happened and forced the fairy woman to undo her wicked spell. However the two pups could not be changed so Fionn took them into his care. He called them Bran and Sceolan.

They grew up to be swift and beautiful hounds. Bran was small and wise, with more than human understanding. She was Fionn's favourite hound. He gave her a collar of gold to wear and led her on a silver leash.

One day, when Fionn and his men were out hunting, a fawn started up before them. They chased it till men and dogs were tired, all except Fionn, Bran and Sceolan, who followed the fawn into a deep valley.

Suddenly the fawn stopped and lay down. Bran and Sceolan knew at once that it was an enchanted creature. They gently licked its face and neck. Fionn was surprised but trusted the wisdom of his hounds and did not harm the fawn.

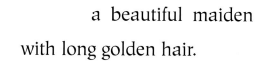

He turned to go back to the castle of the Fianna and the fawn followed. As they passed through the gates of the castle it turned into

a beautiful maiden with long golden hair.

"My name is Sive," she explained. "The Dark Druid changed me into a deer for refusing his love. But here in the castle of the Fianna I am free of his power."

Fionn fell in love with Sive and she became his wife. For a whole year they were together. Then Fionn had to go away to wage battle against an enemy of Ireland.

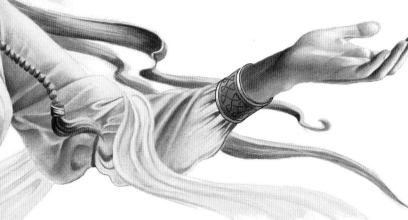

4

While he was gone, Sive watched for his return. One day she saw a cloud of mist coming towards the castle and in the mist she thought she saw Fionn with Bran and Sceolan at his heels.

She ran out to meet them. The mist opened. The Dark Druid, not Fionn, was there. Sive tried to turn back but the druid struck her with a hazel rod, turning her into a fawn once again. He set his dogs on her and they disappeared into the mist.

Fionn was heartbroken. He searched for Sive in every part of Ireland. Bran and Sceolan were the only hounds he brought with him because he could trust them not to harm Sive if they found her.

At the end of seven years he gave up the search. Then one morning while he was hunting on the steep side of Benbulben, his hounds raised their voices and raced into a valley. Fionn followed and found Bran and Sceolan driving the other hounds back from a golden-haired boy. Fionn questioned him but the boy could not speak. "We will take him home with us," Fionn said.

Bran and Sceolan loved the little boy and played with him constantly. After a while he learned to speak and told Fionn of a deer whom he loved dearly. He remembered an evil man who would speak to the deer and go away in anger.

At last the angry man struck the deer with his hazel rod and forced her to follow him, leaving the boy all alone in the valley where Fionn had found him.

Fionn realised that this was his son. He gave him the name Oisín which means little fawn.

Years passed but Fionn hoped always to find Oisín's mother. One misty morning he was hunting on Benbulben. Bran started forward, baying at the scent of a deer. Fionn could not see in the mist. He was afraid that the deer was Sive and forgot that he should trust Bran to know. To silence her, he struck her with her silver leash. At first Bran wondered at being struck by Fionn. Then she looked sadly at him and turned away. She ran down the mountainside to the dark lake which leads to the other world and plunged into it. Fionn was sorry for what he had done but he never saw Bran again.

Yet still on moonlit nights Bran and Sceolan can be seen, playing among the thickets, where the castle of the Fianna once stood. And sometimes when the mist of morning covers Benbulben, the cry of a hound in chase echoes from its hidden peak.

# THE SEA WOMAN

There was once a fisherman who was spreading his nets near the seashore one day when he heard a sweet voice singing a strange lonesome song. He looked to see where the singing came from. On a rock at the edge of the waves he saw a beautiful sea maiden combing her long hair and singing.

He saw that she had taken off the magic cap which sea people wear under the water and left it sitting beside her on the rock. He crept up behind her while she combed and sang and, when he was close enough, he seized her in his arms. The sea maiden screamed and struggled but could not escape.

The fisherman carried her to his house and hid her magic cap in the potato pit nearby, so that she could not go back to the sea. The sea maiden was so beautiful that he fell in love with her and took her for his wife.

At first the neighbours wondered where the beautiful woman came from. The fisherman told them that she was washed ashore from a shipwreck and, because she could not speak their tongue and sang such strange songs, they believed him. They noticed that she had a strange way of looking at the sea from time to time, as if she had left something there, but after a while they stopped wondering about her.

One day the fisherman decided to bring his wife to the town. As they drove away from the sound of the sea his wife looked anxiously over her shoulder. Terrified to be so far from the sea, she jumped from the trap and ran back the way they had come.

Years passed and children were born to the fisherman and the sea woman. He grew so accustomed to having her for his wife that he almost forgot how he found her and only remembered when he put his potatoes in the pit each year and saw the magic cap.

One day he went to a fair. While he was gone his wife prepared dinner. She found that there were no potatoes in the creel in the kitchen and, since she could not wait for her husband to come home, she took the creel herself and went to the potato pit. As she gathered the potatoes she saw her cap sticking out from under them. She dropped the creel and pulled out the cap.

For a moment she hesitated. She looked at the small white house which was her home for so long and listened to the cries of her children at play. Then she heard the sound of a wave breaking on the strand and she quickly left the potato pit carrying the cap in her hand.

"Mother, where are you going?" her children called as she ran towards the seashore.

They followed, sobbing, because she would not look back at them. Not until she reached the water's edge did she finally turn and give her children a long lonesome look before putting on the cap and diving into the sea.

The fisherman never saw the sea woman again. The sea woman's children stayed with their father but they sometimes gazed at the sea with a wild lonesome look, as if hoping for a glimpse of their mother. And it was said that neither they nor their descendants ever ate fish, for fear of eating one of their own relations.

# THE CHILDREN OF LIR

Lir was a king of the Tuatha Dé Danann, the fairy race who inhabited Ireland long ago. When his wife died, Lir mourned deeply but was comforted by his love for his children. He had four children, Fionnuala, Aodh, Fiachra and Conn.

After a time he married his wife's sister, Aoife. At first Aoife seemed to love the children, but when she saw how their father loved them she became jealous. She went to a wicked druid and asked for his help. He gave her a magic wand.

Next day she took the children for a drive in her chariot. Fionnuala did not want to go because she had dreamed an evil dream about her step-mother. However, Aoife forced the children to come with her.

She drove to the shore of Lough Derravarragh. There she stopped and ordered the children to bathe in the lake. They were afraid to disobey. As soon as they entered the water Aoife struck each of them with a magic wand and they turned into swans.

"We have done you no wrong," Fionnuala cried, for although she was a swan, she still had the power of speech. "Tell us how long our enchantment will last."

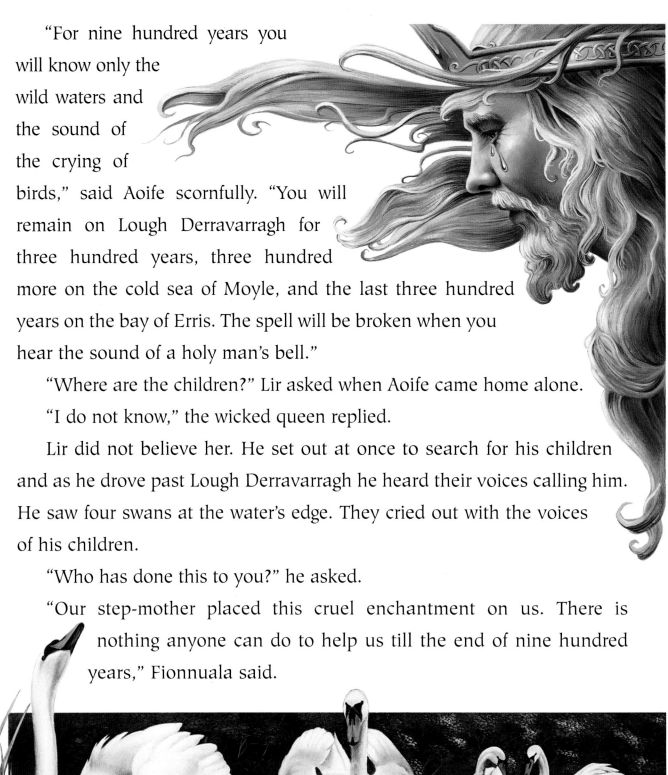

"For nine hundred years you will know only the wild waters and the sound of the crying of birds," said Aoife scornfully. "You will remain on Lough Derravarragh for three hundred years, three hundred more on the cold sea of Moyle, and the last three hundred years on the bay of Erris. The spell will be broken when you hear the sound of a holy man's bell."

"Where are the children?" Lir asked when Aoife came home alone.

"I do not know," the wicked queen replied.

Lir did not believe her. He set out at once to search for his children and as he drove past Lough Derravarragh he heard their voices calling him. He saw four swans at the water's edge. They cried out with the voices of his children.

"Who has done this to you?" he asked.

"Our step-mother placed this cruel enchantment on us. There is nothing anyone can do to help us till the end of nine hundred years," Fionnuala said.

Lir sat all night by the lake and wept. His children comforted him with sweet fairy singing. In the morning he returned to his castle and called Aoife to him.

"You have done wrong," he said. "From this time you will be a witch of the air."

Aoife cried out in terror but Lir's magic overpowered her. She flew up in the air and disappeared, screaming, on the wind.

Lir returned to Lough Derravarragh. Try as he might he could think of no spell to undo the evil enchantment. Years passed and he grew old and grey. People heard of the swans whose song could cure the pain of sorrow and came to listen to them.

At the end of three hundred years it was time for the swans to fly north to the sea of Moyle, a place of black clouds and foaming waves. Fionnuala said, "If we are scattered by storm, let us meet at this rock."

Time after time the swans were dashed apart by the stormy sea. Each time Fionnuala went to the rock and watched for her brothers, who came to her, cold and exhausted. She sheltered Fiachra and Conn under her wings and put Aodh under the downy feathers of her breast.

They remained for three hundred years on the sea of Moyle, lashed by storm and frozen by sharp

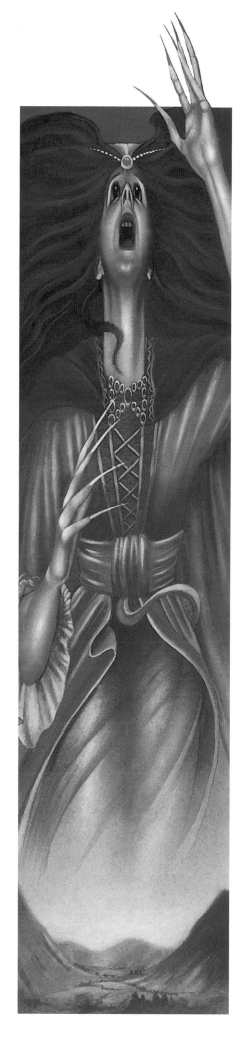

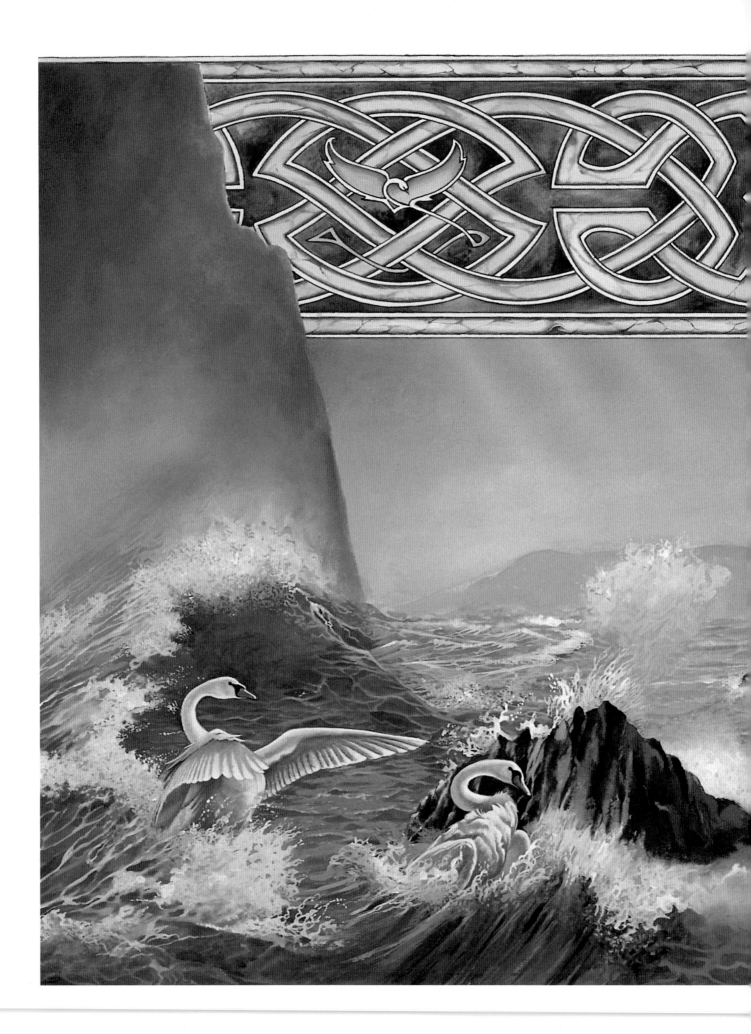

ONE BY ONE
THEY CAME TO HER
COLD AND WET

north winds. Then they flew west to Erris where the west winds drove the waves against the rocky shore forcing the children to seek shelter in the frozen bay. They stayed there for three hundred years until at last they were free to leave.

"Let us fly home to our father," Fionnuala said. Eagerly they flew across Ireland to the hill where Lir's castle had stood but found only a green mound overgrown with thistles and nettles. They knew then that their father and the friends of their childhood were gone.

Heartbroken, they flew away. As night fell they came to a small island on a lake and stopped there. They sang their fairy songs and the birds came to listen to them.

In the morning they were startled by a strange sound. "It is only the chapel bell of a holy man," said the birds.

The children sang their sweet songs till the holy man heard them and came to listen. They told him they were the children of Lir. He brought them to his hut to care for them and had slender chains of silver made to hang about their necks. The children of Lir lived happily with the holy man, glad that their years of sorrow were ended.

# how Cúchulainn got his name

When Cúchulainn was a boy his name was not Cúchulainn, but Setanta. By the time he was five years old he was skilled at playing hurling with his stick and ball, and at fighting with his toy shield and spear. He loved to hear talk of Eamhain Macha, where his uncle, King Conor Mac Nessa, had his castle. The stories of Conor's warriors, the Red Branch Knights, made him long to go to Eamhain Macha and join the sons of kings and nobles who went there to learn the skills of war.

Not long after his fifth birthday he asked his mother, "Which is the road to Eamhain Macha? I want to go there."

"Not yet," his mother said, "you are too young."

"Where is Eamhain Macha?" Setanta asked his father. "Is it east or west?"

"Neither, it is in the north."

Setanta took his hurley stick and ball and went towards the north, playing as he went. Each time he hit the ball he flung the hurley after it, then ran to catch both stick and ball before they landed on the ground.

Soon he arrived at Eamhain Macha. He was delighted to see boys playing hurling on the playing field before Conor's castle. He ran to join their game but the boys stopped playing.

"Who is this stranger who comes uninvited into our game?" they asked.

19

"We are the sons of kings and nobles. Only the son of a king or a noble may play with us."

They tried to drive Setanta away by attacking him with their hurley sticks. Setanta fought back and held his ground against all of them.

King Conor looked out and was surprised to see the small boy defend himself against so many. "Who is that boy?" he asked. "Bring him here."

Setanta was brought to him. "Who are you?" Conor asked.

"I am your sister's son, I have come to play games with the other boys and to learn to be a warrior."

"You are very young," Conor said. However, he gave permission and sent messengers to his sister to let her know that he had taken her son Setanta under his care.

Once the boys knew who Setanta was, they were glad to let him join in their games. One day King Conor passed by the playing field on his way to visit his blacksmith, Culainn, who had invited him to a feast. He stopped for a moment to watch the game and was pleased to see that, although Setanta played alone against all the other boys, he won every game.

He called Setanta and said, "Come with me to the feast at Culainn's house."

"First I must finish my game. Then I will follow you."

King Conor went on his way and arrived at Culainn's house. When the company were seated, Culainn asked Conor, "Is this all who have come with you?"

Conor forgot his invitation to Setanta. "Yes, this is all."

Culainn unchained his hound. Culainn's hound was the largest and fiercest dog in Ireland. Nobody dared approach Culainn's house while his hound was on guard.

Meanwhile Setanta ended his game. "Stay and play another game," his companions pleaded, but he remembered his promise to the king and set off following Conor's chariot tracks and playing with his hurley stick and ball. As he drew near to Culainn's house the hound came bounding towards him, its mouth gaping wide. Setanta flung his ball down the hound's throat. Then he wrestled the dog to the ground and dashed its head against a stone.

Inside, Conor heard the angry snarls of the hound and remembered his invitation to Setanta.

"Quickly, Culainn," he shouted, "call off your hound. That is my sister's child!"

The men leaped up from the table and rushed outside. They found Setanta unharmed and the great hound lying dead at his feet. Cheering, they lifted him on their shoulders. "Put me down," Setanta said when he saw Culainn bowed sadly over the body of his hound.

"Do not be sad," he said, "if there is a pup of this hound anywhere in Ireland, I will find it and train it for you."

"But who will guard my house until then?"

"I will be your guard," Setanta promised. Culainn was satisfied.

"We will call you Cúchulainn, hound of Culainn," said King Conor's men.

"But I like my own name," Setanta protested.

"The name Cúchulainn will be famous in Ireland for ever," said the wise druid Cathbad who could see into the future.

"Then I will be proud to take that name," Setanta said and from that time forward he was known as Cúchulainn.

# OISÍN IN THE LAND OF YOUTH

One morning Oisín, his father Fionn and the Fianna were hunting. There was dew on the grass and the hawthorn was heavy with blossom. They stopped to rest on a hillside and saw a cloud of mist come towards them.

The mist drew near and out of it rode a beautiful woman on a white horse. Her hair was golden, hanging in soft tresses to her waist. The horse's shoes were made of gold and small golden bells tinkled on its bridle.

"Who are you?" asked Fionn.

"I am Niamh, daughter of the king of Tír-na-nÓg, the Land of Youth. I have come because I love your son Oisín." She turned to Oisín. "Will you come away with me to the Land of Youth where there is neither sickness nor death, only happiness and pleasure for ever?"

"Oisín, do not go," said Fionn, but he saw that Oisín loved the maiden. Oisín embraced his father and each of the Fianna in turn. Then he mounted the white horse and rode away with Niamh.

They rode across the white waves of the sea, through magical mists where Oisín glimpsed visions of monsters and giants.

Soon they saw a land lit with golden sunlight. The sun shone on high castle walls. From afar they heard sweet music and as they approached this land young men and women came to greet them.

Oisín and Niamh were brought before the king and queen who were young and beautiful with shining crowns of gold on their heads. They welcomed their daughter Niamh and received Oisín with honour.
A great wedding banquet was held which lasted
three days and three nights.

Oisín and Niamh went to live in a beautiful palace. They lived happily. There was hunting and sports by day and in the evenings there was poetry, music and dancing so the time passed quickly.

Spring came again. The sight of hawthorn in bloom made Oisín think of Ireland. About now the Fianna will be rousing the valleys with the cry of hounds. The dew will be on the grass and the hawthorn will be heavy with blossom, he thought, and longed for home.

"In Ireland men grow old and die. Here in Tír-na-nÓg you will be young for ever," Niamh said, but Oisín was not content.

Niamh brought Oisín hunting in the hills and valleys of Tír-na-nÓg but still he longed for Ireland.

"I must go back to see my father, Fionn, and my old comrades of the Fianna," he said.

"They are not there any more. It is a long time since you left Ireland," said Niamh.

"No, it has not been so long," Oisín replied.

At night he could not sleep and paced his room from end to end. When Niamh saw this she called the young men and women to make music and poetry to distract his thoughts but they were not able to distract him for long. He would remember his home and he would be filled again with longing.

One day when Oisín and Niamh were out hunting they came to a dark inlet of the sea. Oisín stopped his horse. Niamh turned back to see why he had stopped and found him looking at a broken spearshaft floating in the water.

"Look," said Oisín. "This shaft was made from the wood of an ash tree. It has come from Ireland." His eyes filled with tears.

Niamh realised that Oisín could not forget. Her heart was heavy. "Take my white horse and go back across the sea," she said. "But do not alight from the horse because if you set foot on Irish soil you will never be able to return to Tír-na-nÓg."

Oisín took the white horse and rode across the sea. Soon he saw the hills of Ireland rising above the sea mist. He rode on to the land and met a group of people coming towards him.

"What news of Fionn and the Fianna?" he called out.

They looked in astonishment at the richly-dressed young man. One of them, who wore a long robe like a druid, spoke.

"Do you not know that the last of the Fianna died three hundred years ago?"

Oisín was angry at what he took to be the answer of a spiteful druid. Without making any reply he rode on to the castle of the Fianna. As he drew near the hill where it had stood, he wondered that he could not see the castle. It must be covered in mist, he thought, but when he reached the top of the hill he found the fallen walls overgrown with bramble and nettles. Then he knew that the days of Fionn and the Fianna were indeed long past. While only a year had passed in Tír-na-nÓg, many hundreds of years had passed in Ireland.

Sadly Oisín turned away. As he rode westward he saw a crowd of men trying to move a huge stone. They heaved and pushed but could not move it.

"Can you help us, tall champion?" one of the men called out to Oisín.

Oisín leaned from his saddle and with one hand he flung the stone away.

The golden saddle girth broke and he slipped from the horse. His feet touched the ground and the white horse galloped away.

As Oisín stood there he felt a change come over him. His sight grew dim and his youthful strength left him. Within seconds he became an old man, too weak to stand. He thought of Fionn and the Fianna and of his beautiful wife Niamh whom he would never see again. His heart broke and, sinking to the ground, he died.

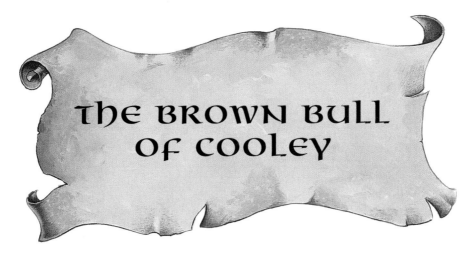

# THE BROWN BULL OF COOLEY

Maeve, Queen of Connacht, was proud and warlike. She liked to boast of her riches and of the many warriors who served in her army. She argued with her husband Ailill that her riches were greater than his.

"You forget that it was I who made you a queen when I married you," said Ailill.

"I had no need of you to make me a queen," Maeve retorted. "I had riches of my own before ever I met you."

They ordered their servants to spread out their possessions so that they could compare them. For every precious jewel which Maeve possessed, Ailill owned one of equal value. For every big iron cauldron in Ailill's kitchen, Maeve had one just as big. Weapons and shields, feather beds and linen were all laid out. They were equal in everything.

They ordered their servants to bring their horses and cattle together and drive them before the castle. Maeve had a horse to match every horse in Ailill's stable and a cow to match every cow he owned.

"But you have nothing to match my white bull of Connacht," said Ailill.

It was true. Maeve had no bull to match Ailill's great white bull of Connacht.

She could not bear to own less than her husband. She asked her warriors, "Where is there a bull to match Ailill's white bull?"

One of them, a man of Ulster, said, "There is a brown bull in Cooley, in Ulster, to match the greatest bull in Ireland."

Maeve sent messengers to Ulster to ask if she might borrow the brown bull of Cooley for a year. Her request was refused.

"I will take that bull by force," she said angrily and prepared to make war on Ulster.

Conor MacNessa and the Red Branch Knights were powerless to defend Ulster. Many years before, the men of Ulster had offended the goddess Macha. She laid a curse on them, that when they most needed to be strong, they would fall into a deep sleep.

Cúchulainn alone was unaffected by the curse because his father was one of the supernatural Dé Danaan people. When Cúchulainn saw Conor and his knights lying in enchanted sleep, he knew that he would have to fight alone against the armies of Connacht.

He attacked Maeve's army silently and secretly, using his sling shot to kill one hundred of Maeve's soldiers every day. One evening as Maeve stood near her tent, with her pet bird perched on her shoulder, a stone from Cúchulainn's sling killed the bird.

Maeve knew that this was a warning. She arranged a meeting with Cúchulainn and they agreed to fight the war by single combat. Each day Maeve sent a warrior of Connacht to fight with Cúchulainn at a river ford. Maeve's army could only advance while her warrior was fighting. When he was killed her army had to halt until the next day.

Cúchulainn hoped, by this means, to delay Maeve's army until the warriors of Ulster would awaken from their enchanted sleep and come to help him.

Maeve however did not keep her word. While Cúchulainn was fighting at the river ford, she sent warriors to Cooley to steal the brown bull and drive it towards Connacht.

Cúchulainn discovered Maeve's treachery and pursued her warriors to the Shannon river, which is the boundary of Connacht, but the brown bull had already crossed over.

The white bull of Connacht was grazing peacefully with his herd when he heard the loud bellow of the brown bull of Cooley. Enraged to hear a rival in his territory, he stamped and tore the ground and bellowed his reply.

The two bulls charged across Connacht to find each other, making the ground tremble with the thunder of their hooves. All day and all night they fought. The rage of their battle echoed on the high mountains, in the deep valleys and across the green plains of Ireland.

Next morning the white bull of Connacht lay dead before Maeve's castle. The brown bull of Cooley stamped the ground and bellowed three times to declare his victory. Then he turned his back on Connacht and went home to Ulster.

Maeve let him go, satisfied now that she and her husband were equal.

# THE SALMON OF WISDOM

The Fianna of Ireland were noble fighting men. Their motto was "Truth in our hearts, strength in our hands, our deeds according to our word."

No man could join the Fianna until he was able to recite twelve books of poetry, defend himself against the spears of nine warriors, run through woods without breaking a twig, leap over a stick the height of himself, pass under a stick as low as his knee and take a thorn from his foot while running.

The chief of the Fianna was Cumhall, father of Fionn. Fionn was only a small child when his father was killed in battle by the men of Clan Mórna. His mother was afraid that Clan Mórna would try to kill Fionn also. She asked two wise women to take him to a safe place and care for him.

The wise women took Fionn to a lonely dwelling deep in the woods of Slieve Bloom. The young boy learned from them all that they knew. They taught him to swim by throwing him into a deep pool and leaving him to make his own way out of it. To make him learn to run swiftly they made him herd hares in a field which had no fence or hedge.

Fionn grew up straight and tall. At last the time came for him to leave the wise women and go to the ancient druid, Finnéigeas, to learn the art of poetry.

Finnéigeas lived in a small cabin beside the river Bóinne. He had chosen that place because it is always beside water that poetry is revealed to poets. Near to his cabin was a deep pool overhung by the branches of the nine hazel trees of wisdom. Nuts of wisdom fell from this tree into the pool and in that pool lived Fiontán, the salmon of wisdom.

It was foretold that whoever first ate of this salmon would possess all the wisdom in the world. Finnéigeas had fished for seven years, but failed to catch the salmon of wisdom. A short time after Fionn came to him he fished for the salmon and succeeded in catching it.

Finnéigeas was delighted. He instructed Fionn to cook the salmon but not to eat any of it. Fionn cooked the salmon with care, turning it over and over. When it was ready he served it to his master.

Finnéigeas saw that Fionn was changed. In his eyes shone the light of wisdom. "Tell me boy, have you eaten any of this salmon?" he asked.

"No master, I have not, but as I turned the salmon I burnt my thumb and put it in my mouth."

Finnéigeas knew then that Fionn had received the wisdom of the salmon. "Here," he said, returning the fish to him, "take the salmon of wisdom and eat it since you have tasted it first."

Fionn ate the salmon and became possessed of all the wisdom of the world. From that time, he had only to bite the thumb which he had burned and he could discover the secrets of hidden magic and see into the future.

"Now you must go away from this place for there is nothing more I can teach you," said Finnéigeas sadly. Fionn took leave of his teacher, and in return for his kindness he made this poem:

How sweet and lovely is May
The blackbird whistles in the living wood
And the cuckoo is singing, singing, singing;
Small bees carry their harvest
Reaped from the flowers;
The harp of the woods plays its music
And the river rushes are whispering together.

*For my mother*

SL


*For my mother, father and family*
*For Moira and Trevor*
Special thanks to Ger

FO'C

SOINBHE LALLY was born in Northern Ireland. A graduate of Queens University, Belfast, she is a playwright, short story writer and a winner of the Hennessy Award. She has written several children's books for Poolbeg including *A Hive for the Honey-Bee* (shortlisted for the Reading Association of Ireland Book Award) and *The Hungry Wind*. She lives with her husband and children in County Donegal.

FINBARR O'CONNOR was born in Cork. He obtained a Higher National Diploma in Illustration at Falmouth School of Art and Design in England. He has illustrated an Irish language book on World Folk Mythology, Irish postage stamps and many book covers. This is his first picture book. He lives and works in Cork.

Published 1998 by Poolbeg Press Ltd
123 Baldoyle Industrial Estate, Dublin 13, Ireland

Reprinted February 1999
Text © Soinbhe Lally 1998
Illustrations © Finbarr O'Connor 1998

The moral right of the author and illustrator has been asserted.

The Publishers gratefully acknowledge the support of The Arts Council.

A catalogue record for this book is available from the British Library.

ISBN 1 85371 829 7

Designed by Poolbeg Group Services Ltd
Set by Poolbeg Group Services Ltd in Hiroshige 14/24
Printed by Dai Nippon, Hong Kong.

# PRONUNCIATION GUIDE

| | |
|---|---|
| Ailill | Al-yil |
| Aodh | Ee |
| Aoife | Ee-fa |
| Bóinne | Bone-ya |
| Cathbad | Kah-bad |
| Connacht | Konn-akt |
| Conor | Konner |
| Conor Mac Nessa | Konner Mock Nessa |
| Cúchulainn | Koo-hul-lin |
| Culainn | Ko-lin |
| Cumhall | Ko-wal |
| Curoi | Koo-ree |
| Dé Danaan | Day Dan-in |
| Lough Derravarragh | Loch Derra-varr-ah |
| Eamhain Macha | Ay-wan Maha |
| Fiachra | Fee-kra |
| Fianna | Fee-yunna |
| Finnéigeas | Finn-ay-gas |
| Fionnuala | Fin-noo-la |
| Fionn | Fee-yun |
| Fionn Mac Cumhaill | Fee-yun Mac Koo-wil |
| Fiontán | Fee-yun-tawn |
| Maeve | Mave (to rhyme with wave) |
| Niamh | Nee-iv |
| Oisín | Aw-sheen |
| Sceolan | Skiu-lin |
| Setanta | Se-tan-tah |
| Sive | Saive |
| Tír-na-nÓg | Cheer-na-n-awg |
| Tuatha Dé Danaan | Too-ha Day Dan-in |